BEATRIX POTTER'S GLOUCESTER

'From the tailor's little booth in Westgate came a gleam of light.' An illustration from Beatrix Potter's original manuscript for *The Tailor of Gloucester*.

BEATRIX POTTER'S GLOUCESTER

A GUIDE TO THE CITY AND
ITS SURROUNDING COUNTRYSIDE

KEITH CLARK

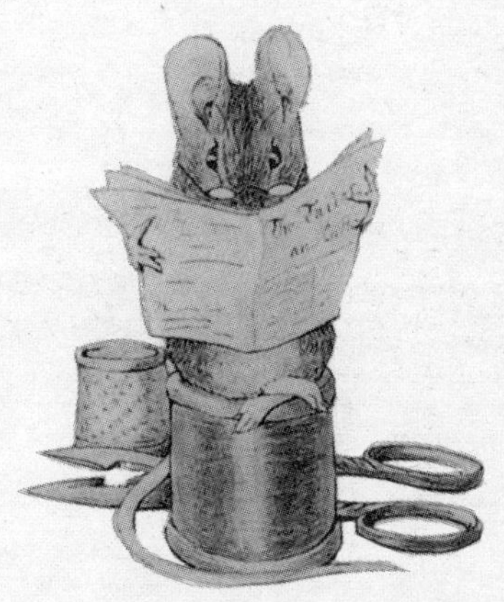

F. WARNE & Co

FREDERICK WARNE

Published by the Penguin Group
27 Wrights Lane, London W8 5TZ, England
Viking Penguin Inc., 40 West 23rd Street, New York, New York 10010, USA
Penguin Books Australia Ltd, Ringwood, Victoria, Australia
Penguin Books Canada Ltd, 2801 John Street, Markham, Ontario, Canada L3R 1B4
Penguin Books (NZ) Ltd, 182-190 Wairau Road, Auckland 10, New Zealand

Penguin Books Ltd, Registered Offices: Harmondsworth, Middlesex, England

First published 1988

Designed by Sue Coley

ISBN 0 7232 3571 6

Printed and bound in Great Britain by
Richard Clay Ltd, Bungay, Suffolk
Filmset in Monophoto 11 on 13 Baskerville

CONTENTS

ACKNOWLEDGEMENTS

The author and publishers are grateful for the following for their kind permission to reproduce the illustrations in this book.

Book Trust (The National Book League), Trustees of the Linder Collection: plate 2 (centre); pages 10 (below), 26 (below), 43 (above), 49 (above), 67 (above), 75 (above)

Stephen Dorey: plate 4 (below)

Mrs Joan Duke: page 55.

The Ford Motor Company: plate 1 (top left); page 43 (centre). The photographs are of costumes in the Victoria & Albert Museum.

Gloucestershire County Library Collection: pages 14, 25 (above), 26 (above), 30 (below), 37 (above)

Alan Sutton Publishing: page 70. This photograph comes from *Stroud and the Five Valleys in Old Photographs – A Second Selection* by S. J. Gardiner and L. C. Padin, 1987.

The Tate Gallery: plates 1 (below) and 3 (above); pages 10 (above), 25 (below), 43 (below), 46 (below), 49 (below), 78.

The Trustees of the Victoria & Albert Museum, National Art Library: page 17 (above).

The Trustees of the Victoria & Albert Museum (Leslie Linder Bequest): plate 1 (top right); pages 10 (below), 17 (below), 21 (above), 46 (top).

Frederick Warne Archive: pages 2, 19, 21 (below), 67 (below), 68.

Derrick Whitty: plates 2 (above and below), 3 (below) and 4 (top left and right); pages 28, 30 (above), 32, 35, 37 (below), 39, 40, 41, 52, 60, 61, 64, 73, 75 (below), 77.

LIST OF COLOUR PLATES

MAPS

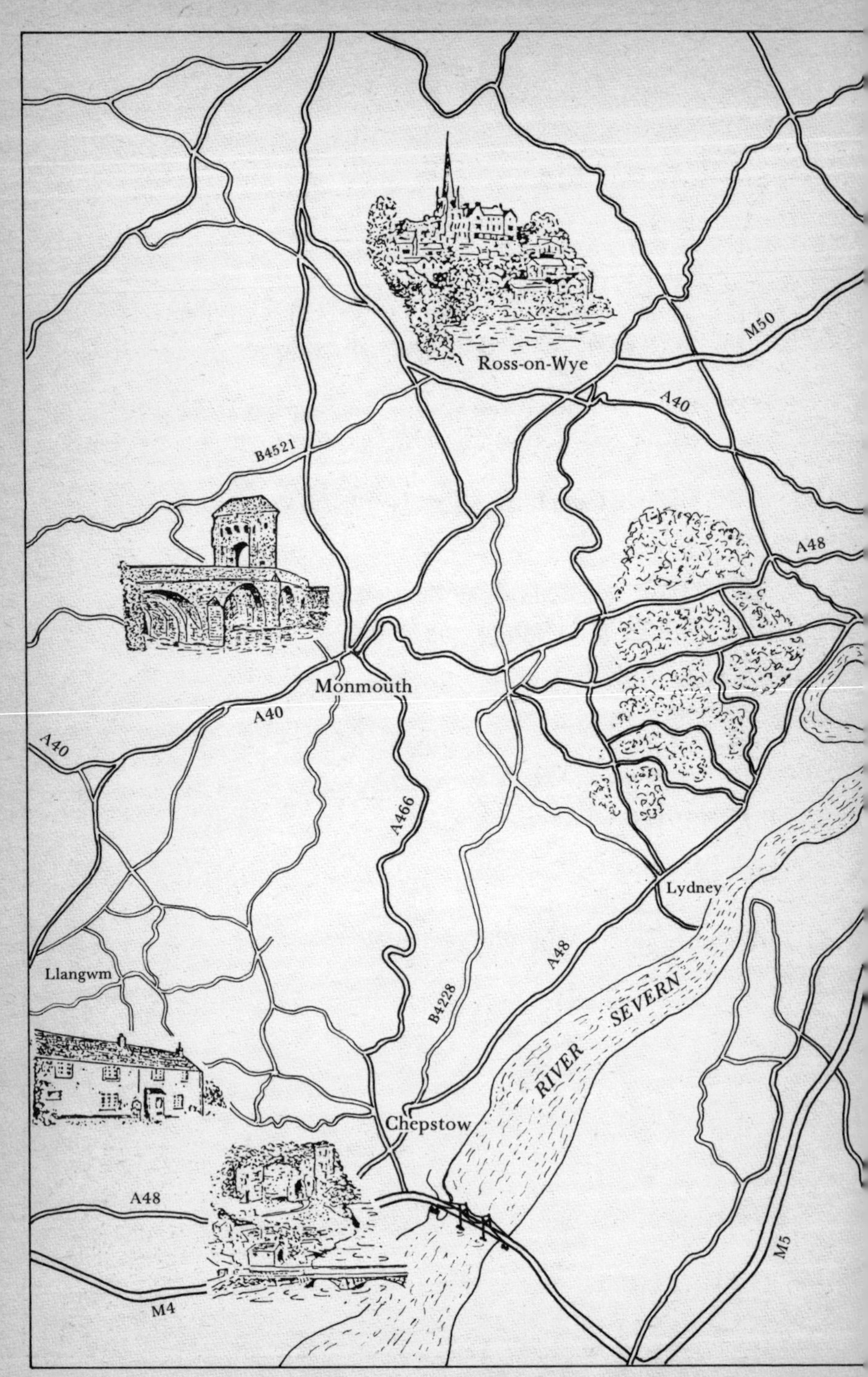

Ross-on-Wye
M50
A40
B4521
A48
Monmouth
A40
A40
A466
Lydney
A48
Llangwm
B4228
RIVER SEVERN
Chepstow
A48
M4
M5

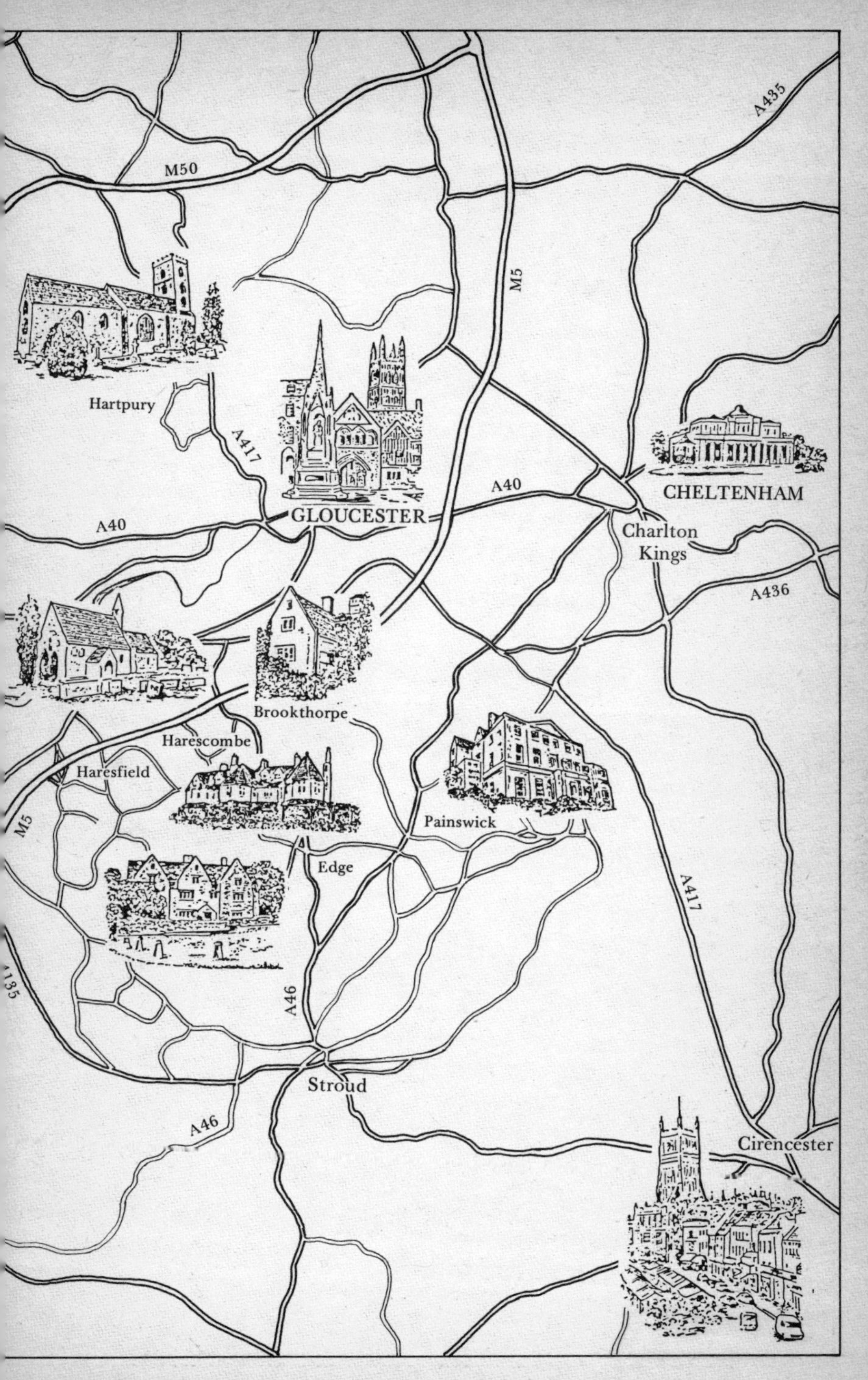
M50
A435
M5
Hartpury
A417
A40
GLOUCESTER
A40
CHELTENHAM
Charlton
Kings
A436
Brookthorpe
Harescombe
Haresfield
M5
Painswick
Edge
A417
A46
Stroud
A46
Cirencester

The bespectacled mouse reading the *Tailor & Cutter*, from the front cover of *The Tailor of Gloucester* (left) was based on a much earlier watercolour called 'The Day's News' (below).

INTRODUCTION

The city of Gloucester has had a long and fascinating history from Roman times: it was, for instance, the city where the Domesday Book was commissioned, where Henry III was crowned, where the body of King Edward II, murdered at nearby Berkeley Castle, was taken to be buried. However, to generations of children all over the world – and their parents – the city is best known not for these major episodes but for a quiet tale about an unnamed, aged tailor and how mice came to his assistance one Christmas Eve. Since Beatrix Potter's *The Tailor of Gloucester* was first published, the origin of the tale, which she stated in her dedication was based on a true story, has intrigued its readers. This book looks at the story behind the book and how Beatrix Potter came to hear it during one of her many visits to Gloucestershire. It also serves as a visitor's guide, pinpointing places associated with Beatrix Potter and with both the fictional and the true Tailor of Gloucester.

Tracing the story and Beatrix Potter's relationship with Gloucestershire will provide quite a journey. It will take you to 'remote' villages and big cities. It will take you through some of the most beautiful scenery in Britain – the Wye Valley, the Royal Forest of Dean, the Tintern Forest, the Severn Valley and the fringes of the Cotswolds. Along the way there is a wealth of places to see and visit – Chepstow Castle, one of the oldest stone-built castles in Europe, the ruined Tintern Abbey, the steam train centre near Lydney, Clearwell Caves, the Regency splendour of Cheltenham and, above all, the bustling cathedral city of Gloucester with its imposing dock-side buildings. It is all there for the adventurous traveller armed with a good map and the spirit to explore. Distances dictate that much of the journey has to be undertaken by car, though there are good rail links between Stroud, Gloucester and Cheltenham and buses from these centres to many of the villages.

Few books are written in complete isolation and this one would have faltered in its early stages without the assistance and support of a number of people. I would here like to acknowledge their help and single out for special mention the Hutton family of Harescombe who have been generous with their help, Farmer Jones of Perthcretig, Mr and Mrs Boddy and others who have allowed their homes to be photographed, the Gloucester County Library, Philip Cooke of Gloucester City Council for his support and Susan Coley for her sensible suggestions and editorial skills.

Keith Clark

I

THE TAILOR OF GLOUCESTER – A HISTORY OF THE STORY

> *My DEAR FREDA*
> *Because you are fond of fairy-tales, and have been ill, I have made you a story all for yourself – a new one that nobody has read before.*
>
> *And the queerest thing about it is – that I heard it in Gloucestershire, and that it is true – at least about the tailor, the waistcoat and the*
> 'No more twist!'

So begins Beatrix Potter's *The Tailor of Gloucester* and our first indication that this, arguably one of the finest books for children ever written, had a basis in fact rather than the fertile imagination of its writer and illustrator.

Quite when Beatrix Potter actually heard the story of the tailor of Gloucester is not known, and unfortunately it is not recorded in her code-written journal although there are entries for several of her visits to Gloucestershire. Original drawings of Gloucester tieing in with the book are known and show that she had the story in mind in 1897, four years before sending the manuscript original to young Freda Moore.

Leslie Linder (1904–1973) noted that Beatrix Potter heard the story of the tailor from her cousin Caroline Hutton, at the Grange, Harescombe, where she often stayed, 'who had it of Miss Lucy, of Gloucester, who had it of the tailor'. The tale, as she heard it, was of a tailor, John Prichard, in the

Westgate Street, Gloucester, in 1897

Westgate area of the city, who had been commissioned to make a suit for the new mayor to wear on his first ceremonial duty, which was heading the procession from the Guildhall in Eastgate to the Shire Hall in Westgate to mark the opening of the annual Root, Fruit and Grain Society Show. As in Beatrix Potter's book, Prichard left some of the work unfinished when he locked up his workshop for the weekend, only to find it almost finished when he returned on Monday morning. One buttonhole was still not sewn, but pinned to the waistcoat was the small note NO MORE TWIST.

A perplexed Prichard placed the finished waistcoat in his shop window with a notice advising 'Come To Prichard Where The Waistcoats Are Made At Night By The Fairies'. Was he delightfully naive or just a shrewd businessman? Whichever is the truth, a legend was then born that has become familiar to generations.

Caroline Hutton also told Leslie Linder that her relation

took little visible notice of the Prichard story, but presumably the idea of turning it into a story (most of the earlier books began as story letters to young friends) was being conceived in her mind, for a couple of days later, when the Huttons and their guest drove into the city, Beatrix Potter asked that the tailor's shop be pointed out. She then, says Caroline Hutton, sat down on a doorstep and began to sketch it. One wonders what her highly respectable, wealthy and typically Victorian parents would have said if they had witnessed the scene. It was a hot summer day, yet Beatrix Potter sketched the street scene in snow! These sketches are almost certainly those in the Free Library of Philadelphia, whose collection also includes Freda Moore's original story letter manuscript. One of the sketches, of College Court, is dated '23–28' and 'Glos.May 97.B.' and on the reverse is noted 'These sketches done in very warm days became the two snow pictures in *The Tailor of Gloucester*.' This may be a very important clue to when Beatrix Potter heard the tale, for she did stay with the Huttons between 23 and 28 May 1897, though after the success of her visit when she found she got on extremely well with her Gloucestershire relations, she became a regular visitor to the county. After one such visit, in May 1903, she wrote to her publisher:

> 'I have had an amusing visit to Gloucester last week, I got a good deal of material in the way of sketches.'

It must have been amusing indeed to walk the streets of the city imagining the antics that 'took place' there that Christmas Eve in the story she was at that time preparing for commercial publication by Warne.

* * *

The Tailor of Gloucester is very much a fairy story, and it was as such that Beatrix Potter described it in the dedication to

Winifred (Freda) Moore (born 8 January 1881), the ten-year-old-daughter of Beatrix Potter's former governess, who received the original story in the form of a handwritten and illustrated exercise book as a Christmas present in 1901. It has the inferred moral and traditional 'happy-ever-after' ending of a good fairy tale, though being Beatrix Potter, mice replace the good fairies and a cat takes on the role of the wicked fairy or evil stepmother who, in pantomime fashion, repents in time to make amends for wicked deeds performed.

It is a book that has many unusual facets, not least that it is the only one of Beatrix Potter's small books to be set in a determinable age, a time 'of swords and periwigs and full-skirted coats with flowered lappets – when gentlemen wore ruffles, and gold-laced waistcoats of paduasoy . . .'

That *The Tailor* began as a story letter written specifically for a young child and not at the request of a publisher, is certainly a contributory factor behind its seemingly everlasting appeal. The story letter beginning was a common origin for a large number of Beatrix Potter's books, and Freda Moore's eight brothers and sisters were all amongst the lucky recipients. Noel Moore, the eldest of the children of Annie Moore, who, as Annie Carter, had been employed at Bolton Gardens to teach Beatrix Potter German and became not just her tutor but also a fairly close friend, received the first of these story letters during an illness in September 1893, when Beatrix Potter was out of town and so unable to visit him in the Moores' Wandsworth home in South London. Noel's was about four little rabbits – 'Flopsy, Mopsy, Cottontail and Peter, who lived with their mother in a sand bank at the foot of a big fir tree' – which Beatrix Potter later borrowed back and rewrote and illustrated to become *The Tale of Peter Rabbit*, privately published for sale to friends and relatives in 1901 and then by Frederick Warne in a commercial edition in 1902.

Winifred ('Freda') Moore
in 1900.

Beatrix Potter made these sketches on the endpapers of one of her privately printed editions. The figure on the right can be glimpsed through the window of the tailor's shop on page 55 of *The Tailor of Gloucester*.

The Tailor of Gloucester was also first published privately at her own expense, but not, as in the case of *Peter Rabbit*, because she had been unable to find a publisher but because she thought Warne would consider it too long and ask for extensive editing, especially of the many rhymes, carols and folk songs. As it was, Beatrix Potter herself cut the story down by well over a thousand words for her own edition and when Warne agreed to publish it they did indeed ask her to edit it by around two thousand words.

Beatrix Potter borrowed the exercise book from Freda Moore and, as we read in a letter to the child dated 6 July 1902 from Laund House, Bolton Abbey, where she was holidaying, the author spent a considerable time rewriting and reillustrating the story for her first printing:

> 'I have kept your picture book a long time and I have not done with it yet; I had to copy out the pictures rather larger and it took me a long time – but you will get it back some day . . .'

Five hundred copies were printed for her by Strangeways and Sons of London and bound in pink paper boards. On 1 December 1902 she wrote to Warne about the book:

> 'Except for the children's rough copy I have not shown it to anyone as I was rather afraid people might laugh at the words.
>
> I thought it a very pretty story when I heard it in the country, but it has proved rather beyond my capacity for working out.'

Although she might have had reservations about the story and her ability to retell it, Beatrix Potter was already beginning to think more highly of *The Tailor of Gloucester* than *Peter Rabbit* or *The Tale of Squirrel Nutkin* which was then being planned for publication by Warne, and certainly more than the small 'jobs' she had executed prior to then – a series of greetings cards for Hildesheimer & Faulkner, a set of nine pen drawings of 'A Frog He Would A-Fishing Go' (an embryonic Jeremy Fisher) for an Ernest Nister annual and six

The Lady Mouse from the original manuscript sent to Freda Moore (*above*), and the current book version.

drawings for a small booklet of poems called *A Happy Pair* by Frederic E. Weatherly. The latter, a great rarity today, has a tenuous link with Gloucestershire, for Weatherly, a solicitor better known for being a noted lyricist (he wrote 'Roses of Picardy' amongst some 200 popular songs) was based in Bristol, then a city and county in its own right whose northern environs were firmly in Gloucestershire, though they are now in the county of Avon.

Beatrix Potter sent a copy of the private edition of *The Tailor of Gloucester* to Warne on 17 December 1902, with the note:

> 'I undertook the book with very cheerful courage, but I have not the least judgement whether it is satisfactory now that it is done.'

Warne however did like it, and on 19 December, Beatrix Potter again wrote to her publisher:

> 'Thank you for your letter about the mouse book; you have paid it the compliment of taking the plot very seriously; and I perceive that your criticisms were just: because I was quite sure in advance that you would cut out the tailor and all my favourite rhymes! Which was one of the reasons why I printed it myself.
>
> I don't mind at all what is done with it in the future; we will see how it goes off this Christmas, and if it is a success it might be improved and reprinted someday. At present it is most in request amongst old ladies.'

After mentioning that she is still working on the illustrations for *The Tale of Squirrel Nutkin*, Beatrix Potter concludes:

> 'I think my sympathies are still with the poor old tailor but I can well believe that the other would be more likely to appeal to people who are accustomed to a more cheerful Christmas than I am.'

The biggest cuts she made for the commercially published Warne edition were in that part of the story where the tailor's cat, Simpkin, wanders the snow-covered streets of Gloucester on Christmas Eve, listening to the singing of the birds and animals, and discovers the mice of the city hard at work in his master's workshop sewing and embroidering 'the most beautifullest coat and embroidered satin waistcoat that ever was worn by a Mayor of Gloucester.' It was a section full of old rhymes and songs – some seasonal carols, others pertinent to the story or to tailoring. These undoubtedly made the central part of the story rather heavy and the tale is far better on the whole for the editing, but it is a section that has considerable charm, as can be seen in the published version of the manuscript.

Not all the rhymes or songs were removed; a number remained, including the very apt:

Three little mice sat down to spin,
Pussy passed by and she peeped in,
What are you at, my fine little men?
Making coats for gentlemen.
Shall I come in and cut off your threads?
Oh, no, Miss Pussy, you'd bite off our heads!

Sung by the mice in the tailor's shop, it is an interesting inclusion, for many years earlier she had toyed with the idea of producing a small booklet around the verse and drew six charming watercolour illustrations, one for each line of the poem. One of these, originally illustrating the line 'Making

'Making coats for gentlemen.' Beatrix Potter's early illustration (*above*) and her reworked version, now on page 47 of *The Tailor of Gloucester*.

coats for gentlemen' was reworked for the Warne edition of *The Tailor*.

Warne published *The Tailor of Gloucester* in October 1903, (the third Beatrix Potter title, as they had issued *The Tale of Squirrel Nutkin* a few months earlier), in an edition of 20,000 copies which, huge though it was for a first printing, quickly proved insufficient, as within a couple of months a reprint of 6000 copies was required to meet demand. After over 80 years, *The Tailor of Gloucester* still sells in enormous numbers as it is discovered by each new generation.

FURTHER READING

Potter, Beatrix, *The Tailor of Gloucester*. Frederick Warne, 1903. Recently reprinted with re-originated illustrations.

Potter, Beatrix, *The Tailor of Gloucester: From the Original Manuscript*. Frederick Warne, 1969.

Lane, Margaret, *The Tale of Beatrix Potter*. Frederick Warne, 1946; revised edition 1985.

Linder, Leslie, *The History of the Writings of Beatrix Potter*. Frederick Warne, 1971; revised edition 1987.

Linder, Leslie (transcribed), *The Journal of Beatrix Potter*. Frederick Warne, 1966.

Taylor, Judy, *Beatrix Potter: Artist, Storyteller and Countrywoman*. Frederick Warne, 1986.

Taylor, Whalley, Hobbs, Baldrick, *Beatrix Potter 1866–1943: The Artist and her World*. Frederick Warne with The National Trust, 1987.

* * *

Some of Beatrix Potter's original illustrations for *The Tailor of Gloucester* can be seen at the Tate Gallery, Millbank, London SW1.

II

GLOUCESTER – THE ACTUAL SETTING

He lived quite near by in College Court, next to the doorway to College Green; and although it was not a big house, the tailor was so poor he only rented the kitchen.

Gloucester is a city that has developed very logically, on the original cruciform pattern set out by the Romans when they established their city of Glevum in the first century AD. From its centre, The Cross, radiate four main streets leading to the entrance gates to the city situated at the main points of the compass – Westgate, Eastgate, Northgate and Southgate. When Beatrix Potter visited it, Gloucester was a thriving seaport with all the cosmopolitan atmosphere that this brings; it still boasts one of the finest surviving Victorian docks, and though its huge brick warehouses no longer serve their original purpose there are exciting conversions taking place, or in the planning stage, to turn these into much desired commercial and residential buildings, leisure centres, museums, etc.

It was also a city of narrow streets and gabled houses and although extensive development has taken place this century to make the compact and busy shopping centre with its roof-top car parking, much of old Gloucester is to be seen in the buildings if you look above the modern shop fronts. Gloucester also boasts many architectural gems that Beatrix Potter would have noticed, like the fifteenth century New Inn in Northgate Street with its balconied courtyard, the Fleece Hotel in Westgate and the medieval timbered Bishop Hooper's Lodgings in Westgate which is now a folk life museum.

It is in Westgate that the main interest lies for the Beatrix Potter devotee, for it was here that she placed the tailor's workshop in Westgate Street itself and his home in a tiny building, 9 College Court, next to the Pilgrim's Gate entrance to the grounds of the magnificent Norman cathedral, where Henry III was crowned in 1216 and where the foully murdered Edward II was buried in 1327.

Number 9 College Court, illustrated on page 39 of present editions, was not always the home of the fictional tailor; in her original manuscript she placed her tailor in nearby Three Cocks Lane, the 'move' to College Court not taking place until the 1903 Warne edition when the illustration of the building and the gateway appears for the first time. Sadly, the real tailor did not live here either; at the time of the book's conception and publication it was the home of the Broadway Oyster Company (1897) and then the cycle depot of H. G. Norton & Co (1905), but nevertheless it will always be the home of the Tailor of Gloucester for most visitors, especially since her publisher, Frederick Warne & Co. bought it in 1978 and converted it into a Beatrix Potter Centre, combining a specialist shop with a small museum devoted to the author and her books.

The street scene on page 16 of *The Tailor* is not to be seen in Gloucester today, but early photographs held by Gloucester Library in their Gloucestershire Collection suggests that this was based on Mitre Street, drastically altered in the early 1930s when it became The Oxbode, today a part of the modern shopping centre, or perhaps on Berkeley Street, another delightful street of gabled medieval buildings sacrificed in modernisation schemes. A drawing by Beatrix Potter in the Linder Collection at the Book Trust (The National Book League) in London of gables and other architectural details could well have been drawn here too.

The illustration on page 40 of *The Tailor* shows a street in which there are two inns – the Crown and the Sun. These did exist in the West Ward of the city, but not in Beatrix Potter's lifetime. According to the Alehouse Licences Records these

An early photograph of Mitre Street which may have been the inspiration for this street scene which appears on page 16 of *The Tailor of Gloucester*.

Beatrix Potter's sketches of gables could have been made from the many medieval houses still to be seen in Gloucester when she visited it; the photograph of Horn Lane dates from 1930.

had disappeared by 1756, so she must have either worked from an old print or it was just one of those happy coincidences.

The address she gave for the mayor, a grocer, in her manuscript and the subsequent privately printed edition also boasted a sign, the sign of the Golden Candle, a detail that was dropped in the Warne edition. Part of the mayor's shop – its cellars – were shown in the earlier versions, illustrating 'In the cellars under the Mayor of Gloucester's shop there was a fine racket! The rats were holding holiday, and dancing the heys, in and out amongst the casks and barrels. (For the Mayor was a grocer, at the sign of the Golden Candle).' The illustration showed the rats having a Christmas celebration and one of them is seen drinking out of a wine bottle, which caused Warne to insist it be dropped for their publication. Beatrix Potter later wrote that she couldn't understand their attitude, and indeed it is a shame for it is a fine illustration, though in such a temperate age perhaps the publisher was wise!

There were as many as eight grocers in Westgate in 1897, none of whom held the position of mayor between 1890 and 1901. One, a J. G. Vicar of 5, Westgate, did have a sign outside his shop, of a golden grasshopper, quite a prominent local landmark in its time and now in the Gloucester Museum. Could this have provided the idea for the sign of the Golden Candle or is it just another coincidence?

The interiors of the tailor's shop were not drawn in Gloucester but in London, in a Chelsea tailor's not far from Beatrix Potter's London home in Bolton Gardens, South Kensington, where she was born on 28 July 1866, and where she lived until 1913 when she married a Lake District solicitor William Heelis and moved to the village of Sawrey. By the subterfuge of pulling off a button from her coat and entering the tailor's to have it repaired, she was able to study the Chelsea tailor at work and note the layout of his shop and the types of tools he used, all later incorporated into the book. She later presented the tailor of Chelsea with a copy of the book and informed him as to what she had done; he in turn showed it to a representative of the *Tailor and Cutter* magazine which reviewed it very favourably – no doubt especially impressed by the cover illustration of a mouse seated on a reel of cotton reading that very same trade journal. Her method of ensuring accuracy in the tailor's shop was typical of Beatrix Potter's thoroughness, which makes an elementary mistake in the illustration on page 15 all the more puzzling; for, although illustrating the text on the facing page 'The tailor came out of his shop at dark . . .' the view through the shop window and doorway clearly shows that it is still daylight.

The frontispiece, depicting a couple leading a wedding procession, has an interesting history. For this illustration an old engraving by William Hogarth called Noon provided her inspiration, a rather bizarre choice because the original showed a couple leaving church surrounded by some rather distasteful scenes. Of course Beatrix Potter radically altered this and typically even managed to insert a cat into the background to ally it closer to the story.

Bishop Hooper's Lodgings: now a folk museum.

VISITOR'S GUIDE

Gloucester has changed considerably this century but there is much remaining that Beatrix Potter would have seen on her visits to the city and a number of direct associations with both the real and the fictional stories of *The Tailor of Gloucester*. As the city is built on a crossroads it is not difficult to find ones way round and there are car parks strategically placed in and around the city centre. For convenience we start this walk from the large coach and car park at the junction of Westgate Street and Royal Oak Road.

1 St Nicholas Church Norman and Roman features, leaning spire.

2 Bishop Hooper's Lodgings A fine Elizabethan building housing a fascinating folk museum illustrating the crafts and industrial, agricultural and social history of the area.

3 Shire Hall The destination of the procession from the Guildhall to mark the opening of the annual Root, Fruit and Grain Society Show, for which the real mayor of Gloucester is said to have commissioned his new suit from the Gloucester tailor. Beatrix Potter would have noted the impressive facade with its early nineteenth century portico, but of course the huge extension is very much post World War Two. The impressive nature of the Shire Hall is not surprising; it was designed by Sir Robert Smirke, architect of the British Museum in London.

4 Three Cocks Lane The home of the Tailor of Gloucester in the original manuscript that Beatrix Potter sent to Freda Moore, and in the privately printed edition.

5 College Street The main road to the grounds of the cathedral and possibly the road that Beatrix Potter used when she visited the cathedral with the Huttons. It has not always

College Street today (above), and College Court, drawn in 1894 by Ed. J. Burrow for the SPCK.

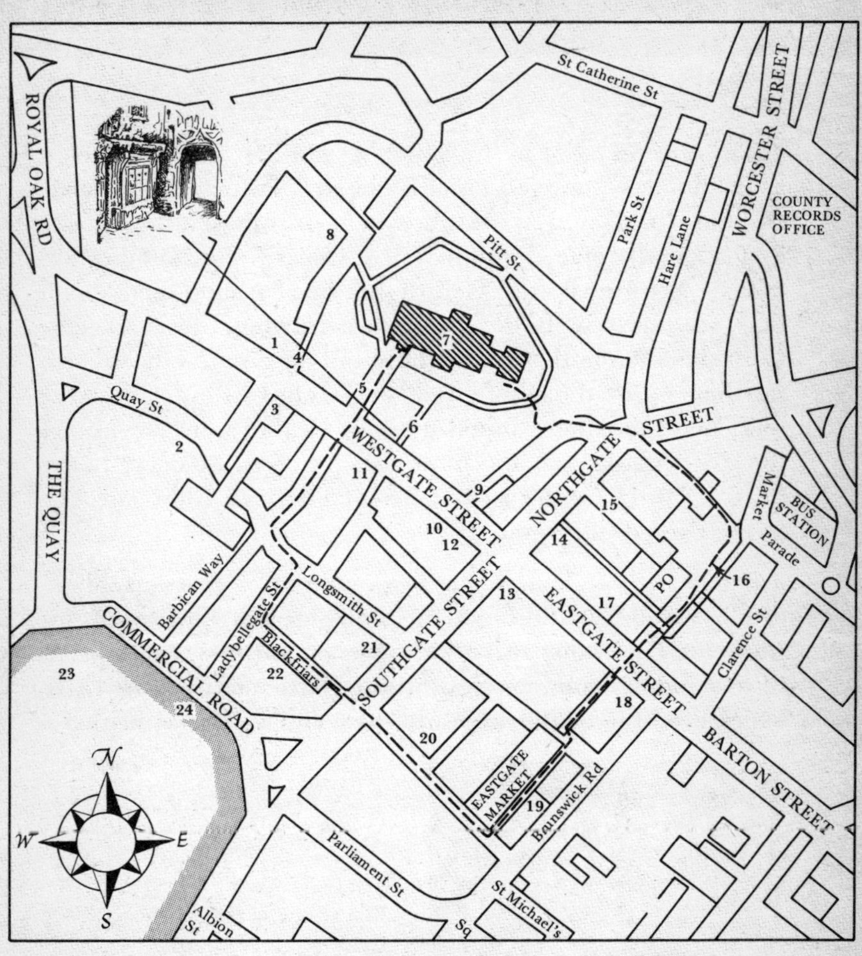

1 St Nicholas Church	9 St John's Lane	17 Guildhall
2 Bishop Hooper's Lodgings	10 The Fleece Hotel	18 East Gate
3 Shire Hall	11 Number 23 Westgate Street	19 City Museum
4 Three Cocks Lane	12 Number 5 Westgate Street	20 Greyfriars
5 College Street	13 The Cross	21 The Golden Cross Inn
6 College Court	14 The New Inn	22 Blackfriars
7 Cathedral	15 The Oxbode	23 The Docks
8 Bishop Hooper's Monument	16 The Via Sacra ----	24 The Custom House

been such a wide road; until the 1890s it was actually quite a small lane.

6 College Court The tiny shop at number 9 was depicted as the home of the aged tailor by Beatrix Potter in the Warne edition of 1903 and in all subsequent printings, although she had originally placed him in Three Cocks Lane. Number 9 is now a Beatrix Potter Centre housing a shop and small museum. Beatrix Potter's original drawing shows College Court lined on both sides by shops but for decades the eastern side has consisted of a dull, red brick wall. In 1987 shops were built here, making a much more agreeable scene for one of the city's best known and most visited streets. Adjacent to the Beatrix Potter Centre is the ancient Pilgrim's Gate entrance to the cathedral grounds.

7 Cathedral A magnificent example of Norman architecture with later additions including a thirteenth century transept. The choir, also a Plantagenet addition, contains an East Window, commemorating the Battle of Crecy in 1346, which is said to be the largest in the country. The cathedral is

The House of the Tailor of Gloucester: the Beatrix Potter Centre in College Court.

PLATE 1
'. . . a cream coloured satin waistcoat – trimmed with gauze and green worsted chenille – for the Mayor of Gloucester.' Beatrix Potter's sketches of this waistcoat in the Victoria & Albert Museum formed the basis for the illustration on page 57 of *The Tailor of Gloucester*.

PLATE 2
Harescombe Grange today and (*right*) part of the garden, sketched in watercolour by Beatrix Potter on one of her visits to the Hutton family. She also visited Harescombe church (*below*).

PLATE 3
'Simpkin . . . came out of the tailor's door, and wandered about in the snow.' College Court as it appears on page 39 of *The Tailor of Gloucester* and today; the tailor's house is now a Beatrix Potter Centre.

PLATE 4
The Fleece Hotel (*left*), dating from the sixteenth century, and (*below*) the New Inn, built around 1450, can both be seen in Gloucester today.

Bishop Hooper's monument, with the cathedral in the background.

of course a must for every visitor, as it has been for centuries, many coming as pilgrims to see the tomb of the murdered Edward II. In the grounds are some notable buildings, including Church House in which Henry VIII slept in 1535.

8 Bishop Hooper's Monument In St Mary's Square, reached from the cathedral grounds through St Mary's Gate. A nineteenth century monument marking the spot where Bishop John Hooper was martyred under the orders of Mary I in 1555. The remains of the stake at which he was burned to death are to be seen in the Folk Museum.

9 St John's Lane The real tailor, John Samuel Prichard, had his workshop at 10 St John's Lane in 1902.

10 The Fleece Hotel One of Gloucester's oldest inns, dating from the sixteenth century but with a twelfth century barrel-vaulted cellar, once part of an earlier house on the site.

11 Number 23 Westgate Street The workshop of John Prichard in 1906. According to research carried out by A. H. Done (manuscript in Gloucestershire Collection at Gloucester Library), 23 Westgate Street prior to *c*1920 was opposite the entrance to College Court, where number 45 is now located.

12 Number 5 Westgate Street J. G. Vicar, mayor of Gloucester, had a grocery shop in 1897 at 5 Westgate Street with a prominent sign of a golden grasshopper. Could this have been the inspiration for the mayor of the original manuscript – a grocer at the sign of the Golden Candle? From the same source as above, 5 Westgate Street in Beatrix Potter's time was opposite the entrance to St John's Lane, where number 9 is to be found today.

13 The Cross The centre of the city and the meeting place of the four major roads to the gates of the old city wall. The tower is all that remains of the Church of St Michael and now houses a well-placed Tourist Information Centre.

14 The New Inn The New Inn in Northgate Street was built around 1450 to house pilgrims to the shrine of Edward II in the cathedral. The timber gallery running round the courtyard is delightful and much photographed by visitors to the city.

15 The Oxbode Today a modern street leading to the pedestrianised Kings Square and from here to the large shops and shopping centre in Eastgate Street. In Beatrix Potter's time however this was a street of medieval buildings with overhanging first floors and a higgledy-piggledy roofline and it appears to have been the inspiration for the illustration on page 16 of *The Tailor of Gloucester*.

16 The Via Sacra A pedestrian walkway created in the 1960s around the city centre roughly following the line of the old city walls.

17 Guildhall The starting place of the procession to the Shire Hall for which the mayor of Gloucester commissioned his new suit from John Prichard.

18 East Gate Underground excavations show sections of the city's Roman and medieval defences, the dungeon of a medieval tower and a stone-lined moat – the remains of the City East Gate which stood up so proudly to the cannons of Charles I and defeated them after a month of battering. Open May to September only, Wednesday and Friday 2pm–5pm, Saturday 10am to 12 noon and 2pm to 5pm.

19 City Museum A Victorian building, open all year round, housing a good collection of artefacts relating to Gloucester from the Ice Age to the present day. First class art gallery.

The Cross

20 Greyfriars Remains of an early sixteenth century Franciscan Friary, destroyed after the Dissolution. Today with a Georgian facade over its west end.

21 The Golden Cross Inn A rambling Elizabethan building in Southgate Street, once the home of Robert Railkes, born in Gloucester in 1735, the founder of the Sunday School movement. There is a statue to Railkes in the Park. Southgate Street has a number of exceptional buildings, including number 9 with its carved Jacobean-style timber facade and an unusual jewellers near The Cross dominated by almost life size automated figures of an Englishman, a Scotsman, an Irishwoman and a Welshwoman who hit large bells in front of them, while a central Father Time tolls the hour by pulling a bell rope fixed to a hammer that hits a great bell hanging beneath an ornate clock.

22 Blackfriars A Dominican Friary and possibly the best preserved of its type in the country. Noted for its impressive original timber scissor roof. Open to the public Monday to Friday 9.30am to 4.30pm.

23 The Docks Gloucester has been a port on the tidal River Severn for centuries but it was the opening of the Gloucester and Sharpness Canal in 1827 that turned it into a prosperous dock city. Enlargement occurred throughout the nineteenth century, with the building of new docks and the large dockside warehouses. The docks declined but are still used for some commercial purposes and for leisure craft mooring. The surviving nine warehouses are finding new uses – one is a museum devoted to packaging and advertising, another is now an antiques centre.

24 The Custom House Now a museum devoted to the history of the regiment of the Glorious Glosters, open Monday to Friday 10am to 5pm.

South of the town, in the industrial Linden area is Tuffley Crescent, off Tuffley Avenue, Bristol Road, where Ida Prichard, the second wife of John Prichard, moved after his death.

Gloucester Docks in 1890 (*above*) and today.

III

THE REAL TAILOR AND THE MODEL

But although he sewed fine silks for his neighbours, he himself was very, very poor – a little old man in spectacles, with a pinched face, old crooked fingers, and a suit of thread-bare clothes.

Beatrix Potter drew her tailor as a poor, aged man, far removed from the real tailor who inspired the story, for John Samuel Prichard was young and the owner of a very thriving business employing at least two apprentices and with a very high reputation amongst the business community of the city.

John Prichard, known to friends and family as Jack, was born on 7 February 1877, not in Gloucester but on the other side of the River Severn, at Perthcretig in Llangwm, a tiny village off the B4235 Chepstow to Usk road in Gwent that is actually two communities – Llangwm Uchaf and Llangwm Isaf. He was the third son of Mary Jane (née James) and Philip George Prichard, both from families well established in the area, there being numerous James' and Prichards' buried in the thirteenth century church of St Jerome in Llangwm, including John James of Perthcretig (1848–1913), Samuel James (1859–1889) and Thomas Prichard (d. 1915).

Philip Prichard, the tailor's father, was a farmer who, it seems, was forced to leave his farm in the 1890s, probably due to the drastic slump in corn prices that occurred then, and seek work elsewhere. He and his family moved to that part of Gloucestershire between the Severn and the Wye, to Primrose Hill in Lydney, a small town on the southern border of the Royal Forest of Dean and close to the Severn on which it once boasted a thriving port and ship building yards. Here

Perthcretig, the birthplace of the real tailor

the former farmer found work, not on the land but in the then prosperous Lydney Tinplate Works, though he subsequently moved to Cheltenham and eventually returned to the land, as a farm bailiff.

His son Jack took a tailoring apprenticeship with Watts of Lydney, a leading and still extant local company, moving to Gloucester some time in the mid-1890s to set up his own business. According to his widow and second wife Mrs Ida Eugenie Prichard, (*Gloucester Citizen*, 16 January 1962), his shop was on the corner of College Court and Westgate Street, though contemporary directories list two other addresses – Number 10 St John's Lane in 1902 and 23 Westgate Street in 1906.

Prichard quickly built up a flourishing business and became quite prosperous and by 1902, when still only 23 years old, he had already become the treasurer of the prestigious Gloucester and Cheltenham Masters and Foreman Tailors' Society. The master tailor eventually sold his business and became a teacher at Hardwicke Reformatory, a school established by the Lloyd-Baker family in the village of Hardwicke with the aim of rehabilitating boys from poor backgrounds who had committed petty crimes. Referring to directories for 1910 and

Prestberries, the home of the tailor's first wife

1914 we find Prichard living at The Gables, Hardwicke.

Prichard married twice. On 3 October 1907 he married Martha Ellen Williams, daughter of Evan Williams of Prestberrie Farm (now called Prestberries) on the outskirts of Hartpury near Newent on the A417. They married at the parish church of St Mary The Virgin, Hartpury. Prichard divorced his first wife on 20 December 1915, citing a Joseph Edwin Welch as co-respondent. One story has it that the co-respondent later became Mayor of Gloucester, but research has not backed this up. It has also been suggested that high legal costs involved in obtaining the divorce caused Prichard to sell his business to become a teacher, though his deteriorating health is just as likely a reason, or that Prichard, a staunch supporter of the local Labour Party, simply felt that helping to rehabilitate young offenders by teaching them his craft was a worthwhile way in which to use his skills.

He died on 24 February 1934 aged only 57, the cause of death being pulmonary tuberculosis for which he had been receiving treatment at Standish Hospital. At the time of his death he was living at 1 Ashley Cottages, Charlton Kings, a village on the outskirts of Cheltenham. It was in Charlton Kings, at the Horse Fair Cemetery (grave number 35, section 2) that he is buried, the kerbstone on his grave actually bearing the incised inscription 'The Tailor of Gloucester'.

Some idea of Prichard's standing in the community can be gained by the fact that on his death the Cheltenham-based *Gloucestershire Echo* not only published a death notice but, on 28 February 1934 carried his obituary on the front page. It was also reprinted in full in the weekly sister paper *The Cheltenham Chronicle and Gloucester Graphic* (3 March 1934, p. 3).

The obituary was headed 'The "Tailor of Gloucester". Death At Charlton Of Man Portrayed In Book' and in this we read:

> 'Mr Prichard was well-known and honoured among a wide circle of friends for the exceptional powers of thought and insight which he brought to bear on human affairs, for his penetrating ideas and for his humorous understanding.'

After noting how an incident in his life inspired Beatrix Potter's book, the obituary concludes:

> 'Those who treasure their memories of Mr Prichard's personal life and conversation know that "The Tailor of Gloucester" is a strangely fitting memorial of a wise and gentle life.'

The tailor must have been a very young man, perhaps not even out of his teens, when the event occurred that was to immortalise him, which would cast certain doubts on the

The tailor's grave in the Horse Fair Cemetery at Charlton Kings.

background to the story except that it has always been substantiated by members of his family, by his obituary and by the inscription on his grave. Regrettably Beatrix Potter never mentioned him or the original 'factual' story in her writings, so the many unconfirmed aspects of the history lack clarification. However, in a letter, dated May 1903, Beatrix Potter wrote to her publisher that on a recent visit to Gloucester she had found that the tailor had now discovered who had completed the waistcoat.

In the interview with the *Gloucester Citizen* reported in 1962, Mrs Prichard stated that it wasn't the mayor's waistcoat that was 'made at night by the fairies' but instead the waistcoat of a three-piece suit ordered for the procession by another local councillor. She stated that the mayor and many of the civic dignitaries had commissioned suits from Prichard and in order to complete the most important – the mayor's – he had asked one of the councillors if he could do without his waistcoat until after the procession. He had however already cut out the councillor's material and it was this, and not the mayor's which had been completed but for the one buttonhole that weekend. This would explain how Prichard was able to place the item in his shop window with the notice, which would surely not have been possible if the waistcoat had been urgently required by the city's mayor?

There is no record of any official uniform or robe having been ordered for a mayor at this time so it was presumably a private commission for a conventional three-piece suit. It is interesting, though more than probably purely coincidental, that the corporation minutes for 19 May 1899 record a resolution to order a dress uniform for the mayor's officer, John Arthur Barnes, though no mention is made of the name of the tailor commissioned to carry this out. The Mayors of Gloucester during the years in which the Prichard story could have occurred were: Albert Estcourt (1895–6 and 1897–8); James

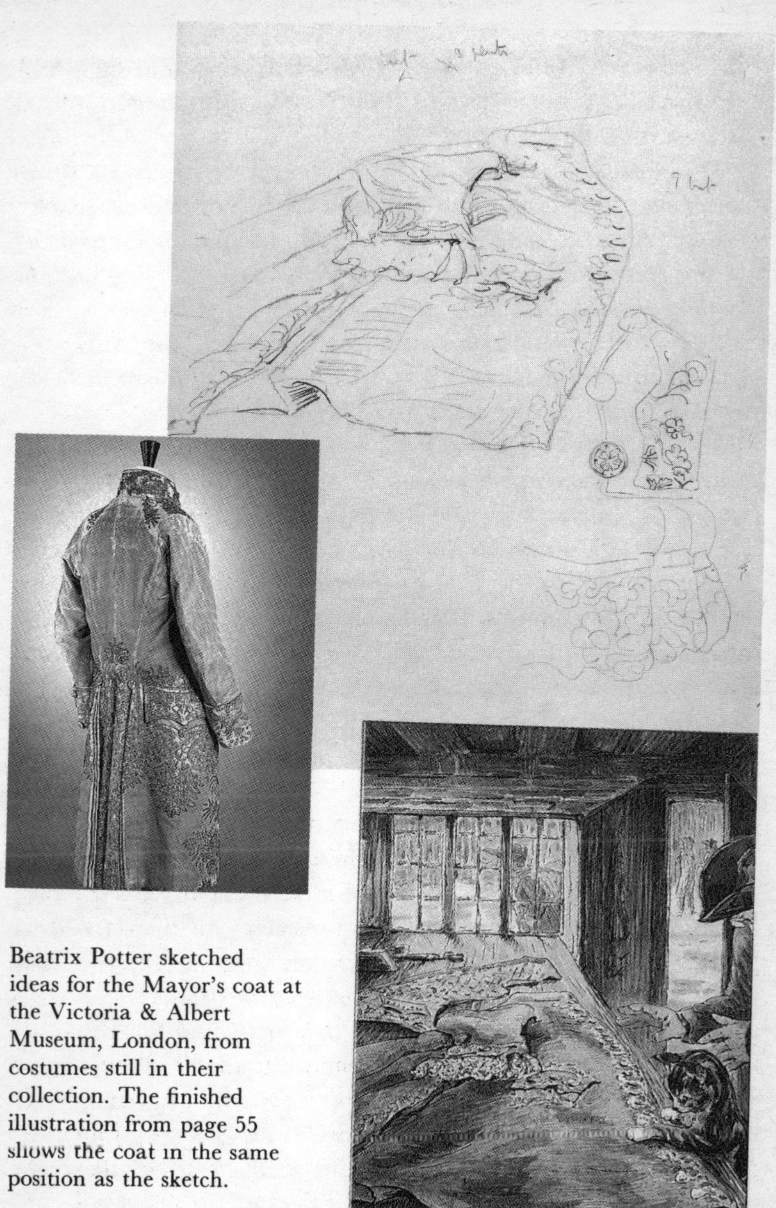

Beatrix Potter sketched ideas for the Mayor's coat at the Victoria & Albert Museum, London, from costumes still in their collection. The finished illustration from page 55 shows the coat in the same position as the sketch.

Brewer Karn (1896–7); Henry Richard James Braine (1898–9); Frank Treasure (1899–1900); Albert Buchanan (1900) and Samuel Bland (1901–2).

Douglas Prichard wrote to Margaret Lane in 1979 and confirmed his mother's story and Beatrix Potter's biographer related this and some new information in an article published in the *Daily Telegraph* 19 March 1979. Douglas Prichard for instance states that it was the annual Lord Mayor's Show rather than an agricultural show for which the suits were ordered but, more important, he casts more light on how the waistcoats were completed that weekend.

It was of course neither Prichard's fairies or Beatrix Potter's mice who worked in the workshop in the tailor's absence; all sources confirm it was his employees. Mrs Prichard had already made it known that two of her husband's apprentices had returned to the shop to help out their overworked employer, but Douglas Prichard tells a slightly different and much more amusing story as to why they returned to the shop after it had closed for the weekend. According to the information he gave Margaret Lane, Prichard's workmen had got rather too drunk that Saturday night and, unable to get back to Quedgeley where they resided, they let themselves into the shop with a spare key to sleep off their excesses. When they awoke on the Sunday morning they were too embarrassed to leave the shop, for the churchgoers were passing by the shop in their Sunday best clothes, on their way to the cathedral, while they were still in their working clothes and still unshaven – not a very good advertisement for a tailor's business. To pass the time until it was dark enough or quiet enough for them to sneak home, they finished the waistcoat and left the mysterious note. They didn't let their employer know what had occurred, presumably out of embarrassment, and it was some years later that the tailor learnt who had really written NO MORE TWIST.

From an article in the *Gloucester Citizen* of 15 April 1971, we learn how Prichard's second wife found out about the relationship between Beatrix Potter's book and her husband:

> 'Mrs I. E. Prichard, who is now 72, still remembers the day she learned that the story was based on her husband before they were married. Having read how the mice came at night to sew a waistcoat Mrs Prichard was expounding her father's theory that the story was not in fact based on truth but an advertising stunt. Her husband corrected her and admitted "I was the tailor".'

* * *

The tailor of Beatrix Potter's version of the 'fairy-story' was depicted as a very old man, even though John Prichard was in his early twenties when *The Tailor of Gloucester* was published. The person who actually modelled for the tailor illustrations, however, was even younger than Prichard – a Gloucestershire boy under ten years of age.

Beatrix Potter found a model necessary because she was not so much at ease drawing people as she was animals and landscapes. She once wrote that she couldn't invent, only copy, and this is a seemingly rather modest and slightly ridiculous statement on the surface for an artist with such an obviously highly developed imagination. However, Beatrix Potter, it is true, invariably used actual and often easily recognisable places for illustration settings and her pets (or those of friends and relatives) and later her farm animals 'modelled' for Peter Rabbit, Benjamin Bunny, Mrs. Tiggy-winkle, Jemima Puddle-duck and the host of other much loved animals that inhabit her books. Beatrix Potter was generally a rather poor artist of the human body, as is clearly shown in her Mr and Mrs McGregor in *The Tale of Peter Rabbit* and the doll-like Lucy in *The Tale of Mrs. Tiggy-Winkle*, and it is likely that this was because she had few close companions she could watch closely or comfortably ask to be models.

Sketches of young Percy Parton posing for the tailor. These were successfully translated into pictures of the aged tailor illustrating 'He sat in the window of a little shop in Westgate Street, cross-legged on a table, from morning till dark', and 'The tailor was very tired and beginning to be ill. He sat down by the hearth and talked to himself about that wonderful coat.'

The elderly tailor did however need an actual model and instead of asking a person of the right age group, which such a shy person as Beatrix Potter may have found too difficult, it was a young boy, Percy Parton, who sat for her.

Percy (1890–1954) was one of the four children of William Parton (died 1925), the coachman at Harescombe Grange. The Parton family lived on the Huttons' estate in a cottage in the wood about three hundred yards from the Grange. Some years later Crompton Hutton had two further cottages built and when Percy Parton married it was into one of these that the couple moved, the other being occupied by a butler. Percy's sister Dorothy (also known as Doll and Doris) became a cook and married the farm bailiff. Brother Herbert (Bert), who married a servant at a neighbouring house, tragically died with his wife while driving home one day in the floods when their gig left the road at Maisemore, turning over and also drowning the horse and their dog.

Percy Parton became the estate gardener, something that stood him in good stead when the First World War broke out for, according to Robert Hutton, Percy proved his worth to the army, which he joined in 1914 at the age of 24, 'on the strength of his knowledge of horses due to his having led the mowing pony at Harescombe Grange.'

The young boy spent many hours sitting for Beatrix Potter, who photographed him as well as sketching him for the tailor drawings. One result was the sheet containing two wash drawings of the boy seated cross-legged on the floor and slumped in a chair, now in the Victoria and Albert Museum collection. The former was used for the illustration on page 8 showing the tailor seated on his work bench, one of the most accomplished paintings in a book containing some of Beatrix Potter's finest work, yet for some unexplained reason this picture was omitted from the privately printed edition even though it had been in the manuscript and was brought back for the Warne edition. The picture of Parton slumped in a chair became the tailor wearily sitting in the chair in front of his kitchen range on page 20 of modern editions, illustrating 'The tailor was very tired and beginning to be ill. He sat down by the hearth and talked to himself about that wonderful coat.'

To make the boy look more like the aged tailor as she envisaged him in her mind, Percy Parton wore a pair of glasses belonging to his father's employer for these sittings.

Percy Parton's daughter, Mrs May Bennett of Cashes Green, Stroud, relates how her father and his sister Dorothy used to take their rabbits and kittens to the Grange for Beatrix Potter to draw, and says of her father's role as model for the Tailor of Gloucester:

> 'He was very proud to tell me, when I was a child, how he used to go to the coach house, or "tack" room I think it was known as, and sit for long periods on a table, cross-legged, while Beatrix Potter drew sketches of him. In my childhood days, to me the Tailor of Gloucester WAS my father.'

The dresser depicted in the tailor's kitchen in a number of illustrations also has a connection with the Grange, as it is believed to have been modelled on one in the Huttons' home. In the Linder Collection at the Book Trust (the National Book League) there is a watercolour of an identical dresser and some crockery on which the artist has noted: 'Tailor of Gloucester, Harescombe?' Beatrix Potter also drew on the furniture and interiors of the Grange, and cottages in and around Harescombe, Edge and Stroud for fireplaces, an old settle, a four poster bed and other items to be incorporated into illustrations.

Not all the illustrations have a Gloucestershire association. The kitchen range on page 20 of the modern editions was, for example, based on one at Melford Hall, the Suffolk home of

Beatrix Potter's background sketch for the dresser which appears on page 19 of *The Tailor of Gloucester* was probably modelled on one at Harescombe Grange.

another cousin, Stephanie Hyde Parker. The longcase clock illustrated in two of the pictures is similar to, if not the one to be seen at Hill Top, the Lake District farm she purchased in 1905 and which, like so many thousands of acres of farmland and hill side as well as farm houses and cottages, she bequeathed to the National Trust. It may be that this clock once graced her London home. The finely embroidered coat and waistcoat were based on costumes studied at the Victoria and Albert Museum, London, where they, and a huge collection of original Beatrix Potter drawings and pictures, are housed. The delightful bespectacled mouse reading the *Tailor & Cutter* magazine on the cover of *The Tailor of Gloucester* was based on a much earlier watercolour called 'The Day's News'.

VISITOR'S GUIDE

John Prichard's story begins in a small village in what at that time was Monmouthshire, but is today the Welsh county of Gwent. What better place to start our journey? From here we follow his life story across the Wye to Lydney and across the Severn to Gloucester, where he made his name. His ties with that city are detailed in another section, but we follow him to Hardwicke, where Prichard taught the young criminals in a reformatory and then to a small village on the outskirts of Cheltenham where his story ends.

Llangwm Ucha, Gwent John Samuel Prichard was born on 7 February 1877 at Perthcretig, a small hilly farm nowadays of around 26 acres set back off the lane between Llangwm and neighbouring Llansoy.

Llangwm is an unusual place, consisting of two parishes, Llangwm Ucha and Llangwm Isaf, with two churches only some 500 yards apart. It has a history of Christian worship over at least 12 centuries. The church of St Jerome at Llangwm Ucha is situated in a valley surrounded by tall trees and hilly farmland. The building is thirteenth century with later additions and has one of the finest carved screens and rood loft to be found anywhere in Wales. In the churchyard are a number of interesting graves: of Thomas Prichard (d. 1915) of Pentre Farm and John James of Perthcretig (1848–1913). The other church, at Llangwm Isaf, is dedicated to St John.

Lydney From Llangwm we follow the family across the Wye to Lydney in the Forest of Dean and on the bank of the River Severn. This journey can be made either through the Wye Valley, past Tintern Abbey, across the Wye at Brockweir and through the Forest of Dean, or to Chepstow, past the castle and over the old iron bridge and on to Lydney following the Severn.

The Prichard family moved in the 1890s to the Forest of Dean, to Primrose Hill, Lydney, where Philip Prichard took a job at the now defunct Lydney Tinplate Works, while his son John took an apprenticeship with a local company, Watts of Lydney.

From Lydney the family split up, the father to Cheltenham and John Samuel's story to Hartpury. For geographical reasons, we take the latter route, travelling through the glorious countryside of the Forest, with its woodland walks, scenic drives and picnic sites and a number of places of interest, including the steam train centre at Parkend, Clearwell Caves and Castle and the town of Coleford, to the A4136, through Mitcheldean to the A40 and then, on the outskirts of Gloucester, take the A417 through Maisemore where Bert Parton, the brother of the boy who modelled for the illustrations of the tailor, his wife, dog and horse died in severe floods.

Hartpury On 3 October 1907, John Prichard married

Hartpury Church

Martha Williams of Prestberrie, Hartpury. Prestberrie Farm is at one end of this scattered rural community, on the lane towards Blackwells End and Oridge Street. At the other end of the village is the church of St Mary the Virgin, where John Prichard and his wife-to-be passed through the notable fifteenth century carved oak porch on their wedding day. Opposite the church is the 50ft long tithe barn, one of the largest in the country. It is a little in need of repair today and sadly disfigured by the corrugated roof linking it to adjoining farm buildings, but nonetheless very impressive for all that.

In the churchyard is the tomb of Mrs Prichard's parents: Evan William (d. October 1907) and his wife Eleanor (d. July 1905). From Hartpury, the next step geographically is Gloucester, but in this section we divert to Cheltenham.

Cheltenham Philip Prichard, the tailor's father moved from Lydney to the ultra-elegant spa town of Cheltenham where he is recorded as living at Pemberton, Albion Street, close to the town centre (off North Street). Prichard returned to the land eventually as a farm bailiff, though no further details are known.

Cheltenham is a town that any visitor to the region should visit, for it is justly famous for its tree-lined Regency streets and upmarket shops. It became a spa town when mineral springs were discovered in 1718 on land now covered by the famous Cheltenham Ladies' College. The market town became a fashionable spa that attracted a Royal seal of approval in 1788 when King George III came to take the waters. The Regency property speculators turned it into a beautiful town of elegant buildings, lovely squares and wide streets. Since that time the town has continued to attract visitors from all over the world, especially in October when it holds an annual and very prestigious literary festival.

Quedgeley The home of the tailor's apprentices. They were unable to return here from Gloucester one Saturday night because they were too drunk, so they stayed in the workshop and completed the important commission.

Hardwicke South of Gloucester. Through ill health or perhaps the cost of gaining his divorce from his first wife, John Prichard, who was a founder member of the local Labour Party, gave up his business and took a teaching post at Hardwicke Reformatory, set up in 1852 by Thomas Barwick Baker in a labourer's cottage on the Hardwicke Court Estate. The reformatory closed in 1922. In contemporary directories, Prichard is listed as living in 1910 and 1914 at The Gables, Hardwicke.

Charlton Kings When John Prichard died in 1934 he was living at 1 Ashley Cottages in the village of Charlton Kings on the outskirts of Cheltenham. He is buried in the cemetery in Horsefair Street (not the churchyard of St Mary's which is in the same street) and the stones around his grave bear the inscription 'The Tailor of Gloucester'. The tailor is not the only literary association of which this once small village can boast. Mrs Craik wrote some of her Gloucestershire-based classic, *John Halifax, Gentleman*, while at Detmore House opposite the Duke of York Inn, and Charlton Kings was the Longfield of Mrs Craik's novel, 'The little nest of love and joy and peace, where the children grew up and we grew old.'

IV

THE HUTTONS, HARESCOMBE AND THE SURROUNDING COUNTRYSIDE

After tea we went down to Harescombe, down some very steep fields, so steep that Caroline pulled me up again with a walking stick. There is a very little old church at the bottom with a curious belfry and a handsome Saxon font, rescued from a ditch.

Beatrix Potter first visited Gloucestershire in June 1894 at the invitation of a 'remote cousin', Caroline Hutton (1870–1958), related to the children's writer by way of her great grandmother (Mary Crompton) having been the sister of Beatrix Potter's great grandfather (Abraham Crompton). Caroline lived at Harescombe Grange, a large country house on the A4173 some three and a half miles from Stroud and five miles from Gloucester, with her parents Crompton and Sophia Hutton and her elder brother Stamford and younger sister Mary.

This visit is described at some length in Beatrix Potter's Journal, from which we learn much about the Huttons and Caroline in particular. In many ways, Caroline Hutton seems almost the opposite of her cousin. Beatrix Potter was a rather plain and reserved young woman with strong, conservative views and something of a serious and introspective nature. Her cousin, who was four years her junior, was on the other hand a pretty, vivacious girl, much more self-possessed and confident, more worldly in a naive sort of way, more outspoken, something of a feminist who (then) did not believe in marriage and decidedly more radical in her thinking.

Beatrix Potter, who was extremely fond of her cousin despite their obvious differences, wrote of her: 'The keynote of her

Caroline Hutton.

Beatrix Potter in 1894: this photograph was taken just after her first visit to Harescombe Grange.

character is decision and complete absence of imagination' (*Journal,* June 1894) and the following year 'She has no discretion, but is altogether charming' (*Journal*, 19 June 1895). Caroline Hutton features a great deal in Beatrix Potter's life and it is a reflection on the relationship that it was to Caroline Hutton that Beatrix Potter turned for advice when marriage was proposed in 1913 by William Heelis.

We have to be grateful that Caroline Hutton was a rather forceful young woman well able to deal with the parental opposition from Rupert and Helen Potter to their daughter's proposed trip to Gloucestershire. The then 28-year-old Beatrix Potter wrote in her diary of how she almost didn't make the journey:

> 'I had not been away independently for five years. It was an event. It was so much an event in the eyes of my relatives that they made it appear an undertaking to me, and I began to think I would not go. I had a sick headache most inopportunely, though whether cause or effect I could not say, but it would have decided the fate of my invitation but for Caroline, who carried me off.'

She must have found the atmosphere of Harescombe Grange extremely convivial compared with the quieter, more sedate and more sophisticated life of her Victorian London town house and Beatrix Potter grew very attached to her country relatives.

Of Mrs Hutton (1834–1908) she was particularly fond, writing at great length about her in her diary:

> 'I don't think I ever became so completely fond of anyone in so short a time. An extremely sweet, placid temper, incapable of being ruffled, rather silent or shyly reserved, but with a most merry enjoyment at anything humorous, observant of things in general, and apparently very learned in her own lines, with tact amongst her family and benevolent interest towards strangers. Capable of directing, yet unquestioning under direction, able to

talk and able to be silent, always amiable and never dull. I cannot imagine a disposition more sweet. It is well in this world to discover there can exist a young woman, clever, brilliantly attractive and perfectly well principled, although knowing her own mind, but I cannot help thinking I would sink the whole lump of independence to have anyone so deservedly fond of me as Mr Hutton is of *Sophy*.'

She began by being slightly afraid of Judge Crompton (1822–1910), feeling that she was under cross-examination the whole time, but she soon overcame these fears and 'came to the conclusion that he is one of the kindest of old gentlemen and certainly a character.' He obviously became equally fond of his guest, whom he called 'The busy Bee', a rather apt description for she was indeed a person who liked to keep herself busy and had a great many consuming passions. She was an accomplished painter, a keen photographer, a dedicated researcher into wildlife, especially fungi, and had a keen interest in politics and worldly matters. In later life she became a sheep farmer of considerable note in the Lake District where she made her home, was an ardent campaigner for the British toy manufacturing industry and even produced posters protesting at the 'conscription' of farmers' horses for war use in the First World War, as well as being a major saviour of the Lake District beauty spots and farmlands which she bequeathed to the National Trust.

The Hutton family possess two photographs taken by Beatrix Potter of the judge reading on the verandah, apparently the only photographs extant of the gentleman who had always refused to have his photograph taken. According to Robert Bruce Hutton, the grandson of Stamford Hutton and resident of the Grange since 1980, Beatrix Potter gained at least one of these (of Mr Hutton standing on the steps to the house engrossed in a book) by skilful trickery. The family legend has it that after Crompton Hutton had refused to let

Judge Hutton photographed by Beatrix Potter on the verandah at Harescombe.

her take his portrait she led the conversation around to literary matters. She asked a question of him and while he looked it up (it is thought it referred to either Milton or Shakespeare) in a book from his library she stole the photograph. Also in the family's possession is a silver teapot given as a present by Beatrix Potter to the present occupant's father Robert Crompton Hutton, on the occasion of his wedding to Elfreda Bruce, the youngest of three sisters who used to visit Beatrix Potter in London (see *Journal*, 25 November 1895) and who told her sons that Beatrix Potter's part of the Bolton Gardens house always smelt strongly of the many animals that were kept as pets.

Robert Bruce Hutton gives us an interesting insight into Rupert Potter's attitude to his daughter's literary success. Her father, a barrister by training though he never practised, was a frequent after-lunch visitor on Sundays to the home of Mr Hutton's grandmother, Mrs Bruce, then a widow living with her daughter Elfreda in Airlie Gardens, Camden Hill, London. 'He used to stay for hours and tell the most boring stories but the consolation from my mother's point of view was that when he left he produced his daughter's latest book out of his pocket.'

* * *

When Beatrix Potter left London with Caroline Hutton on her first visit to Gloucestershire on Tuesday 12 June 1894, they travelled by train from London's Paddington Station to Stroud, a town Beatrix Potter described as 'all up and down hill, a straggling country town devoted to brewers and some dye works'. This is strangely the only direct reference to Stroud in her Journal, yet on each occasion she visited Harescombe Beatrix Potter did so via the town and being the nearest large town to Harescombe, as well as the fact that she was keen on exploring the neighbourhood, would also tend to suggest that in fact she saw Stroud quite a few times in the 1890s.

From Stroud, the two travellers made their way to Harescombe by fly, a one-horse carriage driven by the Huttons' coachman, William Parton, whose son, as we have seen, was to play an important role in the illustrations to *The Tailor of Gloucester*. Beatrix Potter was an observant traveller who noticed much on the journey through Pitchcombe and Edge to Harescombe Grange. She recorded for instance that the steep country lane that was then the main road out of Stroud was 'pervaded by a smell of bean fields and mown hay' and that they were carting hay at a farm below Edge Common. She also wrote of the area around Stroud:

'Down in the valley we saw several grey stone mills with gables and little round windows, the mark of the Flemish weavers who settled here in the days of the Duke of Alva.'

Stroud, as was a great deal more obvious then than now, had a thriving woollen industry which arose through the suitability of the waters of the Frome for the dyeing process, and Flemish weavers were 'imported' to bring their skills to the industry. Today, the textile industry has almost completely died out in Stroud, though there is still at least one mill with an international reputation for quality, specialist cloths.

Unfortunately Beatrix Potter's account of her first visit to the Huttons at Harescombe was written on her return to London and therefore tends towards impressions rather than factual notes, so much is missed out. A casual reference to Gloucester Cathedral for instance tells us that she visited the city, but no further details are furnished.

We are given a lot of information however about one particular walk down to Harescombe village taken early one evening. Harescombe is in a valley while the Grange is situated at the top of a hill so steep (one lane from the village

The view of the valley from Harescombe Grange.

St John the Baptist, Harescombe: the 'little scratched figure of a Jackman' and the Saxon font.

to Edge is 1 in 6) that Caroline had to help her city cousin up again with a walking stick. Through the trees one gains superb views over the whole valley from the Grange, views which Beatrix Potter, a more than talented landscape painter, must have appreciated.

In the valley lies the church of St John the Baptist, which Beatrix Potter describes at some length.

> 'There is a very little church at the bottom with a curious belfry and a handsome Saxon font, removed from a ditch. The thing that struck me was the number of elaborately carved gravestones in the long grass, and the little scratched figure of a Jackman in trunk hose with a halberd, which some idle person had scratched on the door lintel, and on the opposite stone the head and long neck of a medieval lady with her hair in side-cushions like Cinderella's proud sister. There was a great iron sanctuary-ring on the oak door.'

The church, with its curious belfry and ancient font (a plain round bowl supported by thirteen clustered pillars) has not changed to any marked degree since Beatrix Potter's visit.

Even the scratched figures have survived, happily protected from the elements by a deep porch, though her memory did not serve her too well in this case for the figures are actually in the left-hand stone surround of the entrance door and not the lintel and are one on top of the other. The jackman (a servant or retainer) is the topmost figure and more deeply carved by this 'idle person' than the less well drawn lady and in between the two 'engravings' is another, fainter outline of a masculine leg presumably by the same hand. How strange that such a piece of vandalism, perhaps by a boy sheltering from the weather with nothing better to do, or a servant awaiting his master, should have survived to become an object of historical interest.

To the carved tombs described by Beatrix Potter have been added the graves of Crompton and Sophie Hutton, their unmarried daughter Harriet Mary (1873–1937), their son Stamford (1866–1941) and his wife Helen, née Fenwick (1871–1956). There is also the sad grave of Frances Henrietta Hutton who, in November 1963 at the age of only twenty-four, was killed in a road accident at Painswick just two months after her marriage to Gabriel Bruce Hutton. More recently has been added the joint grave of Robert Crompton Hutton (1897–1978) and his wife Elfreda (1903–1986), in the same style as the earlier graves of the Hutton family – a plain horizontal stone slab on which has been fixed a copper engraved memorial panel.

It was perhaps here that the Huttons attended church, Beatrix Potter writing in her Journal that Mr Hutton 'goes to church once on a Sunday, reads the lesson and sleeps regularly during the sermon' or alternatively, the picturesque church at Edge which is actually slightly nearer Harescombe Grange. It may even have been the much photographed church at Painswick where the vicar, William Seddon, was a close friend of Crompton Hutton. Seddon, vicar of Painswick on two occasions, from 1885 to 1898 and again from 1897 to 1912, was quite a character. He and his wife lived in a large house formerly called Gwynfa which is now the Painswick Hotel and according to the Rev Henry McKinley, some of the older parishioners still remember him from their Sunday School days. A memorial tablet was erected to his memory in the church (as well as a screen on the south side of the chancel), recording the parish's affection for their vicar: 'Young and old, rich and poor, saint and sinners when ever in need found in him a friend. By enlightened teaching and a winning personality he promoted Christian fellowship and raised the life of the parish to a higher level.' Beatrix Potter relates a rather scathing anecdote concerning the red-headed clergyman and his wife (a member of the Perrins sauce family): 'He had just returned with his wife from the Holy Land where they had been round, and Mrs Seddon was obliged to come home because she had no change of clothes.'

The area surrounding Harescombe Church was also described in her Journal:

> 'A few yards further on in an orchard, under gigantic Perry pear trees, were some mounds in the deep green turf, all that is left of a stronghold of the de Bohuns. There were the remains of a moat, but we could not go into the meadow because of a great roan bull feeding quietly with some fine cows.'

The object of the walk was Hayes Farm, a 'large old gabled limestone building with stone-mullioned windows and picturesque chimneys'. Beatrix Potter also noted an old mill with its wheel in place and the cottage of a Sam Fluck, listed in a 1902 directory as a shoemaker, who was descended from Flemish weavers. Typically the entry records incidental observations, such as badger markings discovered in the copse behind the Grange and the fact that goitre occurs amongst the villagers! There is also the record of a late night conver-

Hayes Farm, 'a large old gabled limestone building with stone-mullioned windows'.

sation between the two cousins during which they 'got under the venetian blinds to watch the fires in the forest, coal villages amongst the woods, and then looked across to Stockend Woods under the shadow of Haresfield Beacon. Caroline talked on labourers, their miserable wages of eleven shillings a week, their unsanitary cottages, their appalling families and improvidence.' She would not recognise the village now, for most of the old cottages have been completely renovated, new building has taken place and there is the opulent air of a commuter village – not surprising when one considers the proximity of Stroud, Gloucester and the motorway. That same late night discussion covered the reasons Beatrix Potter had enjoyed the service at Gloucester Cathedral, her only diary reference to her having visited this glorious building and the city as a whole.

This is surprising, but just one of a number of details one would have expected to find in her Journal entry for this visit, omitted perhaps because it was written on her return to

London. We have already seen she wrote little of Stroud and Gloucester and a similar omission is the village of Haresfield which is close enough for Beatrix Potter to have visited and with enough of the sort of attractions to interest her, including the site of Roman and Saxon camps, a hill top stone commemorating the siege of Gloucester in 1643, a fine church boasting a Saxon sculpture and a grave with an epitaph by the poet John Dryden. We know she visited Painswick, attending a garden party at the home of Squire Hyett with the Huttons, yet she makes no mention of the village itself even though it has many fascinating historical associations of the type that is usually mentioned in her Journal, such as the fact that Anne Boleyn stayed at Painswick prior to her execution in the Tower of London.

Beatrix Potter journeyed to the county many times after this first visit but exact details of some of these trips are scanty. Her next visit was in June 1895, still within the period of her journal writing and therefore documented in that invaluable source, when she stayed with the Huttons for ten days, 'a most enjoyable visit which no wise fulfilled my doubt as to the wisdom of repeating a very pleasant experiment. I enjoyed it more than my first one, and did not quarrel with Caroline.'

By 1895 Caroline Hutton was showing signs of a change in attitude: 'That fascinating young person has quitted metaphysics and taken to dancing' writes Beatrix Potter wryly, adding that her cousin was 'developing a taste for society which points suspiciously towards matrimony'.

During the 1895 stay Beatrix Potter attended four tea parties with her cousin and indulged her interests, taking over 30 photographs (she was a keen photographer, as was her father, a quite early photographer of considerable skill who amongst other subjects took photographs of the sitters of Sir John Millais so the Royal Academician could continue to paint their portraits without their continuous presence) and collected many fossils, some of which she photographed in the attic of the Grange. She finishes her entry for this visit: 'I shall probably remember my first visit more distinctly than my second, but it was every bit as pleasant and nothing spoiled.' Caroline Hutton returned to London with her before going on to Wimbledon, to stay with the family of Helen Fenwick, to whom her brother Stamford had just got engaged to be married.

Of her 1896 visit we read in the Journal 'had some pleasant grubbing in Huddinknoll quarries for fungi and triumphantly found a shark's tooth'. Her interest in fungi was especially strong at this time because she had been compiling a large portfolio of fungi drawings, some of which were published in a book on woodland fungi in 1967, and researching in detail the reproduction of one species, the result of which was a paper by her read to the Linnaean Society of London, a noted natural history learned society, in April 1897.

There was another visit to Harescombe in November 1897 and again in May 1903, by which time she was working on *The Tailor of Gloucester* for Warne, having already seen the publication of the privately printed edition, writing to her publisher that she had got 'a good deal of material in the way of sketches'.

We know there was a visit in October 1904 because the date appears on two pen and ink drawings. One is an easily identifiable drawing (in the Linder Collection at the Book Trust) of a farmhouse on the main A4173 Stroud to Gloucester road at Brookthorpe which still looks much as it did when she drew it and had a block made of her drawing, possibly to reproduce as a greetings card. The other pen and ink is a sepia sketch of a ladder stile (Linder Collection) inscribed 'At Harescombe Oct 2nd to 9th. 04' which she used for the background for an illustration to *The Tale of Little Pig Robinson*

The ladder stile sketched at Harescombe in 1904 (*above*) later used as background in *The Tale of Little Pig Robinson.*

(page 37 of the first edition, not published until as late as 1930 but conceived many years earlier).

This illustration to Pig Robinson and the various Tailor pictures were not the only ones with an association with Harescombe and Gloucestershire. During one visit to the Grange for instance she rescued two mice caught in a trap in the kitchen, took them back to London, tamed them and gave them the names Hunca Munca and Tom Thumb – they became the models for her two villainous characters in *The Tale of Two Bad Mice* (1904). One of the rhymes proposed for inclusion in *Appley Dapply's Nursery Rhymes* (conceived in 1905 but not published until 1917) arose from a visit to the Grange. On 3 November 1897, she wrote an illustrated letter from Gloucestershire to Freda Moore, as in some other cases using an alternative spelling of the child's first name:

> 'My dear Frida,
>
> I must tell you a funny thing about the guinea-hens here. You know what they are like, I daresay, grey speckled birds with very small silly heads. One day Parton, the coachman, saw them in the field, running backwards and forwards, bobbing their heads up & down and cackling (they say Pot Rack! Pot Rack! Pot Rackety Rack!). They were watching something white, which was waving about in the long grass. Parton could not tell what it was either so went close up to it, & up jumped a fox! It had been lying on its back waving its tail.'

Part of Beatrix Potter's letter to Freda Moore of 3 November 1897.

This anecdote inspired a rhyme for the original Appley Dapply manuscript omitted from the published edition of 1917:

'Galeny, galeny, galene!
– Now what is *that waving between*
The nettles and docks on the green?
Potracket, potrack, potrack!
The thing wavered forward and back –
Potrack! potrack! potrack!
Then the cowman crossed over the green,
And explained to Galeny, galene!'

Some years later, in 1908, Caroline Hutton was staying with Beatrix Potter at Sawrey when she was writing *The Tale of Jemima Puddle-Duck* and the two spent some time trying to find a suitable spot for the duck's nest illustrations – a patch of rhubarb by the gate to the farmyard was eventually chosen. Caroline was by this time Mrs Caroline Clark, having married Francis William Clark, the Laird of Ulva. They had one son, also Francis William (1912–1944), who, as a major in the Argyll and Southern Highlanders, died in Italy during the Second World War. To Caroline's son was dedicated *The Tale of Mr. Tod*, giving this and, as we have seen *The Tale of Two Bad Mice*, *The Tale of Jemima Puddle-Duck* and *Appley Dapply's Nursery Rhymes* links, though perhaps somewhat tenuous, with Gloucestershire.

VISITOR'S GUIDE

Beatrix Potter began her visits to Gloucestershire by arriving at Stroud and that is where we start this section of the journey, travelling with her along the Gloucester road to Harescombe where she stayed with relations and where she heard the story that was to become *The Tailor of Gloucester*. Like Beatrix Potter, we visit the village of Harescombe, the neighbouring villages and countryside of which she wrote in her Journal and perhaps drew in her sketchbooks.

Stroud Beatrix Potter's visits to the county began by rail from Paddington to Stroud, where the station was built by the renowned engineer Isambard Kingdom Brunel in 1843. Brunel also designed a wooden viaduct to carry his railway at Stroud, but this had been replaced by the present brick structure by the time Beatrix Potter began visiting relatives at

King Street Parade, Stroud, in the late 1890s.

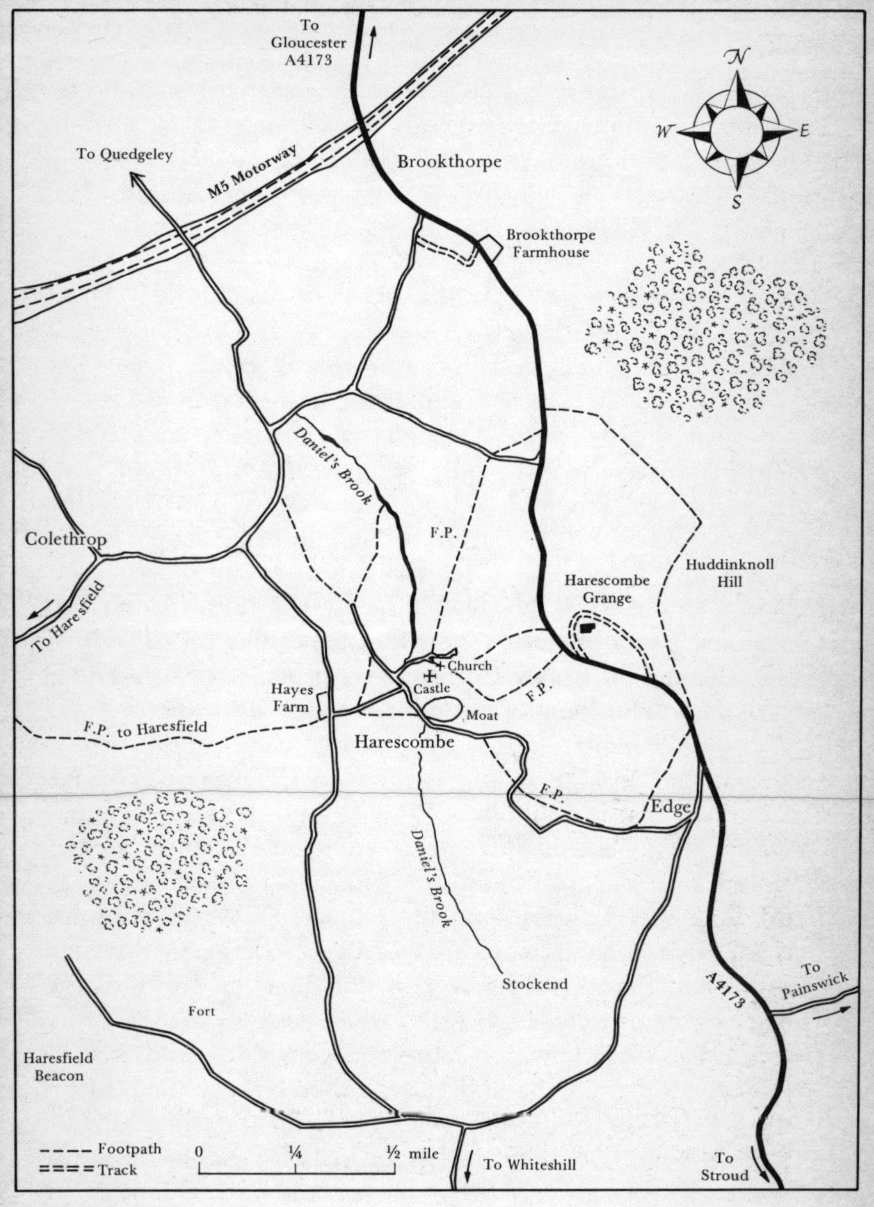
To Gloucester A4173
N
W
E
S
To Quedgeley
M5 Motorway
Brookthorpe
Brookthorpe Farmhouse
Daniel's Brook
F.P.
Colethrop
To Haresfield
Huddinknoll Hill
Harescombe Grange
Church
Castle
Hayes Farm
Moat
F.P.
F.P. to Haresfield
Harescombe
F.P.
Edge
Daniel's Brook
Stockend
A4173
To Painswick
Fort
Haresfield Beacon
Footpath
Track
0
¼
½ mile
To Whiteshill
To Stroud

Harescombe. She describes in her Journal how Stroud is 'all up and down hill'. Its hilly streets are today devoted mostly to shopping but with many elegant reminders, in the form of large houses built for local mill owners, of the days when the textile industry brought prosperity to the town. Stroud Civic Society publishes a useful town walk.

Pitchcombe and Edge Beatrix Potter's journey to Harescombe by road led through the 'Sleepy Hollow' villages of Pitchcombe and Edge. This is a steep hilly journey by car let alone by carriage as she and her cousin Caroline Hutton travelled; the road passes through thickly wooded countryside (the beech trees are especially colourful in autumn) culminating just past Edge Church in a panoramic view over the Stroud Valley and the Severn to the hills of the Royal Forest of Dean, a scene which Beatrix Potter simply described as 'and then there was the view'. Edge itself is off the main road, a pleasing small hamlet of few houses nestling on the side of the hill amid the woods. Cottages here provided Beatrix Potter with models for items of furniture, etc., for illustrations to *The Tailor of Gloucester*.

It is said that an earlier resident of Harescombe Grange requested that the church at Edge be built because he found it difficult to get to the one in the valley at Harescombe! The church is at the crossroads of an old Roman road from Bath to Gloucester Eastgate and the Gloucester-Stroud turnpike road. Edge, though small, has had an interesting history back to Roman times (a Roman villa was discovered in the now National Trust-owned beech woods). Edward IV's army camped on Huddinknoll Hill between Edge and Brookthorpe, on the lane behind Harescombe Grange, in 1471 on the way to the Battle of Tewkesbury; on the same hill the Cavaliers and Roundheads fought in 1644, the Roundheads eventually retreating to Brookthorpe. Rudyard Kipling spent

The kitchen gardens at Harescombe Grange.

holidays at Hilles, the Edge home of Detmar Blow, onetime Lord of the Manor of Painswick and a friend of many artists and writers, including William Morris; in the Second World War, Max Beerbohm stayed at Highcroft, near the present day Edgemoor Inn.

Harescombe Beatrix Potter's relatives, the Hutton family, lived at the Grange, a large and rather splendid house hidden by the trees on the main A4173 but with views of Harescombe village and across the valley to the Severn river and beyond. It is still a private house, owned by members of the Hutton family and not open to the public, with a fascinating mixture of gables and chimneys on different levels, an old fashioned Victorian walled kitchen garden and surrounded by farmland steeply rising behind the house.

Harescombe Village can be reached from the Grange by road from Edge Church or a small turning further down the hill towards Brookthorpe. There is also a footpath to the village – perhaps the one that Beatrix Potter and Caroline Hutton took on their 1894 walk to Hayes Farm? Although small, the village seems to have had a strangely lengthy history and have been of some importance. The establishment of a castle here signifies a strategic value that is far from evident today. In the Domesday Survey, actually commissioned by William the Conqueror at his Christmas Witan or annual court in Gloucester in 1085, the village is listed as Dudestan Hund and later as part of the de Bohun manor of Haresfield. Although the first recorded consecration of a church here is July 1315, a chapel is recorded in a charter of 1181. The parish was originally some 479 acres and it is recorded that the population has changed very little, as far as numbers are concerned, over the past 130 years. However, the way the houses have been altered, and the types of cars in the driveways, shows that the character of the area has changed considerably since Beatrix Potter and Caroline Hutton sat up in bed and discussed the miserable wages of the farm labourers and their unsanitary cottages!

St John the Baptist Church, described in some detail by Beatrix Potter in the Journal, has a curious belfry, a double bell turret over the chancel arch, comprising a small octagonal spire over two compartments for the bells, decorated with smaller octagonal pillars on four sides. The church, which dates back to the thirteenth century, was restored in 1871 and the belfry rebuilt but following the original style. Inside the church is the unusual font noted by Beatrix Potter during her 1894 visit; it is 2ft 6in in diameter, and consists of a drum mounted on 13 small pillars standing on a circular base – all carved from a single block of stone, possibly from Minchinhampton. The scratched figures on the stonework surround to the porch door have survived, though in recent years a less artistic hand has added more graffiti including a very poor copy of the original Jackman 'engraving'. In the churchyard, to the rear of the church, are the graves of members of the Hutton family, including Crompton and Sophie Hutton, with

The farmhouse at Brookthorpe still looks much as it did when Beatrix Potter sketched it in 1904.

whom Beatrix Potter stayed at the Grange, and their children Stamford and Harriet Mary.

Behind the church is a steep hill, the site of a Norman castle built for the de Bohun or de Boun family. The only sign of this today is the moat that Beatrix Potter and Caroline Hutton could not visit because the farmer had his roan bull amongst the cows in that field.

Hayes Farm is a large, three-gabled limestone building as described in the Journal, with signs of having been extensively renovated since Beatrix Potter's visit. It is privately owned and not open to the public. As is quite common with farmhouses, the main entrance is at the rear of the building away from the road.

Huddingknoll Quarry is situated over the hill behind the Grange. It was here that Beatrix Potter spent her visit of 1896 'grubbing' for fungi and records that she also found a shark's tooth.

Brookethorpe In October 1904 Beatrix Potter drew in pen-and-ink a farmhouse on the main A4173 Stroud to Gloucester road at Brookthorpe. It is thought that she subsequently had the drawing printed for use as a private greetings card. The boot scraper set into the bottom of the wall next to the gate in her drawing is not so visible today, being rather overgrown. The timbered building itself has changed very little.

Haresfield As mentioned elsewhere, Beatrix Potter does not seem to have visited Haresfield, the neighbouring village to Harescombe, or at least did not record any such visit in her Journal. She would have found a village with much to offer and one whose history belies its size. The Romans certainly came here, for a sizeable collection of Roman coins was discovered in 1837. The Saxons and Normans also seem to have discovered its strategic value and camped here, perhaps building small settlements. The Siege of Gloucester of 1643 is commemorated on a stone nearby, while the church too offers much historical information. The sculpture figure on one of the buttresses may be Saxon, and the stone figures of two graceful ladies inside the church are possibly members of the de Bohun family who built the castle at Harescombe. The tomb of John Rogers, who died at the age of 11 years, is notable for its verse by the great poet John Dryden. For really superb views over the Severn, Forest of Dean and the Welsh Hills and beyond, a walk up Haresfield Beacon will reward the effort of a steep climb.

Painswick What is now the Painswick Hotel, with its impressive facade, was in Beatrix Potter's time the private residence of William Seddon, vicar of St Mary's, Painswick, and a close friend of Crompton Hutton. It is now an elegant hotel, with a recently built annex.

Painswick, which has been deservedly described as 'The Queen of the Cotswolds' is an extremely picturesque small

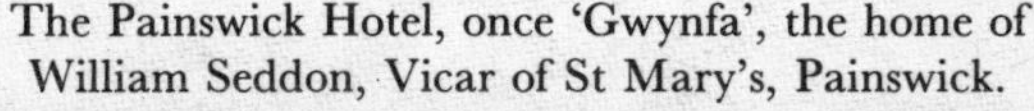

The Painswick Hotel, once 'Gwynfa', the home of William Seddon, Vicar of St Mary's, Painswick.

town, packed with grand scale houses and equally delightful small cottages, and attracts tourists by their tens of thousands throughout the year. The crowning glory of a town packed with architectural gems is the parish church, whose 172ft lean spire dominates Painswick and the countryside around. The 99 well manicured yew trees (there must surely at one time have been a full hundred?) of the churchyard, some of which are over 200 years old, must be some of the most photographed trees in the land. Painswick can have changed little since Beatrix Potter visited it and attended a garden party at the home of the influential Squire Hyett during her 1894 visit.

One of the people she may have met at this garden party was Margaret Hyett who in 1901 designed the bell designs that are carved into the barge boards of the lych-gate entrance to the churchyard of St Mary's.

INDEX

Figures in italics refer to illustrations. B P is Beatrix Potter.